Books by Bill Kincaid
[All are available on Amazon & Kindle]

Ventryvian Legacy
[Science Fiction/Fantasy]

Wizard's Gambit
Kings and Vagabonds

Historical Fiction

Nicodemus' Quest
Saul's Quest
Joseph's Quest
The Making of the President:
The Nightmare Scenario

Humor/Fractured Fairy Tale

Ronald Raygun and the Sweeping Beauty

Drama/Plays

Sweeping Beauty [comedy]
Celestial Court [Christian]

Ronald Raygun

and the Sweeping Beauty

By Bill Kincaid

Ronald Raygun and the Sweeping Beauty is a work of fiction. Names, characters, places and incidents either are the product of the author's imagination or are used fictitiously. Any resemblance to actual persons, living or dead, events, or locales is entirely coincidental, except that some names, places, events, phrases or other items may be used for satire or humor. After all, *fractured* fairy tales are by their basic nature satires of popular or well-known fairy tales.

Copyright © 2013 by Bill Kincaid.

All rights reserved.

Published in the United States of America by Peacemakers Press, 2013.

Additional copies of this and other books by Bill Kincaid are available at Amazon.com

FOREWORD
[You wouldn't really expect it to be BACKWORD, would you?]

A long time ago in a galaxy far, far away...

Wait! That can't be right. Since all the characters in this story speak English, how can it possibly have occurred "a long time ago in a galaxy far, far away?"

All right, let's try this:

𝔒nce upon a time, in a strange and far away land...

That may be a little bit better, but I still don't know about it. Why are fairy tales always set in some far away land? Doesn't anything ever happen around here?

And why is it such a strange land, anyway? Has it been subjected to the rulings of the California Supreme Court?

And why do fairy tales almost always start with the words "Once upon a time" and end with the phrase "and they lived happily ever after?"

I suppose it may be better to be *once upon a time* than it would be to be twice or thrice upon that same time, and it is also probably true that we may not be far enough past Watergate or various impeachment proceedings to begin a fairy tale with the words "At that point in time." Nevertheless, I still wonder why it's done.

For that matter, why is it that whenever a wicked witch disrupts the christening of a baby princess, there is always at least one good fairy remaining who has not used her allotted wish? Is that something the Good Fairies' Local Union insisted on putting into the collective bargaining agreement?

What would be the likely legal repercussions of allowing the manufacture of poison apples (such as the one used by the Queen in *Snow White*)?

Could Rumplestiltskin have sued for breach of contract?

If the Prince in *Cinderella* promised that he would marry the girl whose foot fit the small dainty glass slipper, wouldn't such a promise subject him to the specter of having to marry scores of preadolescent girls whose foot would have fit the slipper? If he went ahead and fulfilled his promise, could he then be charged with either bigamy or polygamy?

If you are like me, the traditional fairy tales may have raised all sorts of similar questions in your mind. Back when I was in high school and college, I would play around with such issues with my oldest nephew, Kent Yates.

Since that time, I have continued fracturing fairy tales and satirizing movies, songs and advertisements with my own children. The story of Ronald Raygun and the Sweeping Beauty began many years ago when Kent and I were producing various satires for our own amusement, continued through bedtime stories with my daughters, and has finally emerged in the form you will find in the pages that follow.

I hope you enjoy it.

Bill Kincaid

This book is dedicated to

Lily Freeman,

who delights her grandparents with her own stories and artwork

Table of Contents

Foreword	5
Cast of Characters	11
Curse of the Wicked Witch	15
Penelope	29
Shyster	43
Vista Ridge	53
The Godfather	67
The Palace Ball	77
The Quest	91

Cast of Characters

Ronald Raygun—Crown prince and most eligible bachelor in the kingdom. Hero and all-around good guy. If this were a Western cowboy movie, he would be the dude in the white hat.

Cole Black Raygun—King and Head Honcho of the Kingdom. Ronald's dad (who is getting impatient with Ron's inability to find the Right Girl to marry, since old King Cole wants to spoil some grandchildren before he dies).

Glorianna Raygun—Queen of the Kingdom. Ron's mother and Cole's wife.

Wicked Witch of the Sand—Rather nasty, bad-tempered old hag who probably got up on the wrong side of the broom.

Princess Anesthesia—Better known as the Sleeping Beauty. Was cursed by the Wicked Witch of the Sand.

Prince Charming—Guy from Survivor Island who gets engaged to Princess Anesthesia.

Princess Penelope—Title character in the Princess and the Pea; also known as Princess Pea-Pea.

Cynthia Ellen Fitzgerald—Better known as Cinderella, the usual title character of the fairy tale. Sweet-natured and uncomplaining housekeeper and general flunky in her own home.

Lord Shyster—The Royal Attorney. Helps the King find Royal Loopholes in laws.

Ophelia Payne—Private courier who delivers the invitations to Cinderella and her stepsisters.

Anthony Lake—National Security Advisor to U.S. President Bill Clinton.

Madeline Nervosa Fitzgerald—Married Cinderella's dad shortly before his death. Primary job is to boss Cinderella around. Would probably wear a black cape and a handlebar mustache if she were a he.

Zirconia and Vampira Nervosa—Madeline's spoiled brats; Cinderella's stepsisters.

Francis Scott Key Fitzgerald—American author during the Jazz Age, a term coined by Fitzgerald.

The Godfather—Cinderella's fairy godfather who comes to the rescue. Would be the knight in shining armor except that it would mess up his hairdo.

Curse of the Wicked Witch

CROWN PRINCE RONALD RAYGUN moved cautiously across the crescent-shaped balcony to a set of double doors. He quietly pressed down on the ornate handle, and it gave way beneath his touch. Raygun pushed on the door, and it opened on silent hinges, revealing an oval room beyond.

Drawing his sword, Ron stepped quietly into the room and looked around. The room was lit only by the ambient light filtering through the doors he had just opened . . . and by light streaming through four slender arched windows on the far side of the oval chamber.

Centered in front of those windows was a bed—and lying on the bed was a young woman. She was richly dressed, wore a coronet on her head, and appeared to be resting peaceably on top of the bed.

Once more Ron examined the oval room and the bed on which the sleeping beauty lay. Finding no sign of traps or snares, Raygun put his sword back into its sheath. He walked to the bed and looked more closely at the girl.

He had expected her to be beautiful—but her beauty exceeded anything he had thought possible. Hair like golden wheat cascaded past her shoulders. Her complexion was like peaches and cream; her skin seemed wondrously soft—yet was supple and inviting to the touch. And those lips . . .

Raygun caught himself wanting to press his own lips against the luscious red lips of the gorgeous maiden lying before him. *"Snap out of it,"* Ron told himself. As inviting and delectable as a kiss might be, that was the last thing he needed to be thinking about at a time like this. One kiss might undo everything. Better finish the job he had come to do.

He gently stroked the girl's cheeks and forehead. She remained in deep slumber—just as he had expected.

Bending over the girl, Ron gently lifted her sleeping body and carried her through the double doors and back out onto the balcony. There he bent down and carefully placed the lady onto a small rug that was stretched out on the crescent balcony. The rug, which was about eight feet long and approximately five feet wide, was an ornate Persian carpet Ron had brought for just this purpose.

No, he mentally corrected himself. That wasn't quite correct. Actually, the carpet had brought him. And now it would take him back—with the sleeping damsel at his side.

Ron sat down beside her, and he quietly commanded the carpet to rise and move forward. Silently it lifted from the balcony and floated through the air.

As they slipped away from the balcony of the high tower in which the maiden had been lying, Ron looked down at the castle that tumbled away far below them. Sentries slept at their posts. Horses and dogs slept in the stables. Nobles and ladies slept along the colonnades, stairways and balconies below, and somewhere in the castle, Ron knew that the king and queen—parents of the girl sleeping beside him—also slept. The legend had been true. Surrounding the castle on all sides was a dense jungle that did not sleep. Oh, no: It was altogether too awake. It was a magic jungle with thorns, brambles, carnivorous plants, and poisonous vines designed to keep away the handsome prince whose kiss could wake the sleeping beauty.

Ron knew the story well. Approximately eighteen years earlier seven good fairies had attended the infant girl's christening. They had bestowed upon the young child all the usual and customary magical traits that good fairies delight in giving on such occasions: unsurpassed beauty, intelligence, sweet disposition, the grace of a flower, the voice of a nightingale, and the gift of making music on any musical instrument she touched. But an uninvited guest had also made her appearance that night.

Just as the sixth good fairy was finishing her gift for the infant girl, a vortex of swirling mist and sand arose before the astonished king and queen, and out stepped a gnarled and loathsome dirty old hag with a long pointed nose and even longer, more pointed fingers.

"Ah, ha, ha, ha, ha!" she cackled. "So you thought you could get by without inviting me, did you?"

"Who *are* you?" asked the queen.

"*What* are you?" muttered the king.

"*I* am the Wicked Witch of the Sand!" trumpeted the old crone.

"The what?" sputtered the king.

"The Wicked Witch of the Sand!" repeated the witch.

The king turned to one of his advisors. "That's not the same as the Wicked Witch of the West, is it?"

"No, Sire," answered the advisor. "The Wicked Witch of the West melted while making a movie some time back. If I recall correctly, the Wicked Witch of the East was also killed while doing the same film when a house fell on her. That was definitely not a good outing for the

Wicked Witches. The liability claims and wrongful death lawsuits were horrendous, as I recall. But this is someone else altogether. Quite frankly, I have never heard of her."

"What?" shrieked the Wicked Witch of the Sand, her face livid with fury. "You've never heard of the Sand Witch? Well, after tonight, you ought to easily remember me. Oh, yes, your little girl will indeed grow to be beautiful and talented and graceful and all the other things these little fairies have wished for her. But before she is fully grown and married, she will choke on a McDonald's hamburger—and she will die!"

Cackling with glee, the Wicked Witch of the Sand stepped back into the vortex of mist and sand—and disappeared.

As the king and queen sat in shocked silence on their thrones, the seventh fairy stepped forward from the shadows where she had been standing. Seeing her, the queen asked hopefully, "Is there anything you can do to nullify what the Sand Witch has done?"

"Alas, no," answered the fairy. "That Witch's power is too great for me to fully countermand her curse—but what I can do for your daughter, I will do."

The fairy walked to the crib in which lay the little baby. "Oh, sweet child," the fairy said. "You will *not* choke on the Sand Witch's hamburger . . . because . . . uh—" and her voice trailed off as she desperately sought for *something* she could do for the poor girl. Suddenly remembering an inspiring childhood fantasy, the fairy's face lit up as she continued, "because before you even have a chance to take a bite, the aroma will so overcome you that you will fall into a deep sleep that will last until—

"Until—"

The fairy muttered something to herself, turned her back on the king and queen, and tapped the air in front of her with her magic wand. A novel suddenly appeared in front of her, suspended in the air. The fairy grabbed the book, flipped through it for a few moments, and apparently found the passage she was seeking.

As she read from the novel, the fairy's countenance brightened and she muttered to herself, "Ah, yes, that ought to work."

She then turned back to the infant and continued her wish. "Before you even have a chance to take a bite of the Sand Witch's sandwich, the aroma will so overcome you that you will fall into a deep sleep that will last until you are awakened by the first kiss of true love from a handsome prince."[1]

All went well for the next seventeen years. Then, shortly after the princess' engagement to Prince Charming (from Survivor Island) was announced, something—or someone—enticed the princess up the long winding stairs to the top of the castle's highest tower. There in the oval chamber at the top of the tower, the princess encountered a Big Mac—and collapsed as if dead. The poor girl didn't even have a chance to try the super-sized Coke and French fries.

---

[1] She was obviously addicted to romance novels and soap operas.

Attracted by a high cackling noise that sounded somewhat like deranged laughter, members of the princess' personal bodyguard found her lying in the oval chamber. Her parents ordered a bed to be brought to the room and had her placed on top of it. Then they sent for the good fairies to see if anything else could be done, and they contacted Prince Charming, since it was hoped that his kiss would awaken their daughter.

Since parents of a pretty girl do not often invite the girl's boyfriend to come over and smooch on their daughter, Prince Charming recognized the invitation as being a Rare Opportunity. And—as everyone knows—opportunity knocks but once. Temptation may keep banging for years, but opportunity only knocks once. Charming therefore left as quickly as he could for the castle. But even as fast as he was, the witch was faster.

When Prince Charming came within sight of the castle, he discovered that the castle had been entirely encircled with a dense jungle of carnivorous plants and poisonous vines. Foolishly believing that his armor (and his love for the princess) would protect him, Charming attempted to hack his way through the jungle—and almost died in the attempt.

He probably would have perished if the good fairies had not rescued him and nursed him back to health. Since they realized that it might be a while before either the princess was rescued or the siege of the castle could be broken, the fairies caused all the inhabitants of the castle to also settle into a deep sleep until the spell on the princess could be broken.

While Prince Charming was still recovering from his ordeal, he remembered Prince Ronald Raygun, a resourceful friend he had met at the Kings, Rulers and Princes' School[2] they had both attended, and he sent a messenger to fetch his friend. Ron returned with the messenger, listened to the Charming explanation, and explored the obstacles that now barred the way to the castle. Among other things, Ronald

---

[2] KRAPS.

discovered poisonous plants, carnivorous coconuts, venomous vines, Slitherin' snakes, hungry Hufflepuffs, galloping Gryffindors and ravenous Ravenclaws. The place was definitely magic, all right. There was no way to get through that magic forest or to go around it. Ron concluded he must find a way to go over it.

Prince Raygun therefore got out his trusty laptop computer, googled several words and phrases, and eventually found a site called Camelot. As is rather obvious from the name, Camelot is a place in Arabia that primarily sells new and used camels. But Camelot also carried a small inventory of flying carpets.

The carpet that now carried Ron and the sleeping beauty safely above the magic forest was purchased from Camelot. Ron guided the carpet to the cottage where Prince Charming was now staying.

"P. R.!" called Charming from the door to the cottage.

"Hey, P. C.!" Ron responded. "I brought your bride for you to smother with kisses and otherwise keep yourself occupied and out of mischief."

"Many thanks," Charming replied, shaking Ron's hand while moving next to the sleeping princess. "I don't mind if I do."

As Charming pressed a kiss to the beautiful girl's lips, she woke with a start. Then, seeing that it was her fiancé, she hugged him tightly to herself and passionately returned his kisses. When Charming eventually came up for air, he saw Ron watching in bemused silence.

"Oh, please forgive me," he gasped. "I suppose introductions would be in order. As I am sure you have surmised, this beautiful young lady is my fiancée, the lovely Princess Anesthesia."

"And this," he nodded at Ron, "is my good friend, Prince Ronald Raygun." Turning to the maiden, Charming added, "He rescued you after I was unable to do so. I almost got killed trying to free you, but Ron was able to get past the magic jungle."

"I was glad to be of service, Princess Anesthesia," Ron said, bowing to the lady. "But I suggest we get back to the castle to let your friends and family know you are all right."

"What about the magic jungle?" asked Charming.

"Based upon what you said about the spells and curses," Ron answered, "I suspect that the jungle should have disappeared now that the curse on Anesthesia has been broken."

Raygun was almost correct. Although the jungle had not disappeared and was still where it had been, it was no longer alive and threatening. It was rather in the process of drying up and crumbling as they passed through, no longer the menace that Prince Charming had previously encountered. Indeed, developers were already making plans for replacing the life-threatening magic forest that had encircled the castle with more user-friendly shopping malls, Starbucks, Wal-Marts and similar wallet-threatening enterprises.

Penelope

PRINCE RAYGUN looked neither to the right nor to the left at the profusion of colorful flowers blooming in their meticulously raked beds, cascading from the carefully pruned bushes, or trailing along ornate trellises. Although he normally enjoyed the waterfalls and fountains of the Royal Gardens, today he hardly noticed them. He did not even bother to breathe in the fragrant smells that filled the morning air.

Instead, Ron kneeled forward and looked intently at the pansies and marigolds in the flowerbed before him. He was kneeling down ostensibly to get a better look at the intense coloration of the flowers—but in reality, he was only pretending to admire the flowers. Ron was actually attempting to escape the notice of others. In other words, the crown prince of the realm was hiding. But he wanted to do it in a socially acceptable manner. If he were caught, Ron didn't want it to appear that he was hiding.

It wasn't that he was anti-social. *Anti-princess* would probably be closer to the truth.

Ron had stayed with Prince Charming and Princess Anesthesia about ten days longer than he had originally planned. It couldn't be helped, he reminded himself. After all, they *had* asked him to serve as best man at their wedding. And he had enjoyed it all immensely. Also, Ron had been required to explain to Green Peace why destroying the magic jungle had been a good thing rather than the ecological disaster they had originally claimed. But still . . .

Still, his absence had upset some of the plans of his parents, who had scheduled several state dinners and parties with neighboring rulers and their families. Ron suspected that it was more than just mere coincidence that each of the visiting monarchs had at least one unmarried daughter reasonably close to his age.

But this wasn't anything new. In fact, the people themselves weren't even particularly new. Prince Raygun had met the various royal families—including the unmarried princesses—several times before. Nevertheless, he had the distinct feeling that his parents were getting desperate.

Parents getting desperate? Whoa! Who did he think he was kidding? Who was currently hiding in the garden pretending to be examining flowers he had seen hundreds of times before?

That's not totally fair, Ron chided himself. After all, he did enjoy the palace gardens, and he did often come here to enjoy the beautiful flowers, trees and waterfalls. It was a very good place to be alone and think. Some days he could—

"Well, hello!" a voice behind him called out cheerfully.

Ron looked around. It was the most recent princess. *What was her name, anyway?*

31

"Oh, hi," Ron stalled as he got to his feet and dusted himself off. *Now he remembered.* "I didn't see or hear you coming, Princess Penelope."

"I hope I didn't disrupt anything, Prince Raygun."

"No, you didn't. I was just looking at some of the flowers."

"They are quite lovely. Do you come here often?"

"Yes, I do. I find the gardens to be peaceful and relaxing."

"Oh, we have so much in common. I also like flowers—and flower arranging."

"Is that a hobby of yours?"

"Oh, yes," she breathed as she leaned demurely toward Ron and gazed up into his silvery blue eyes.

"What other hobbies do you have?" asked the prince as he took a half step backwards.

"I, uh—I like to crochet. And there's also embroidery and etiquette."

"Etiquette? I never considered etiquette to be much of a hobby."

"Well, it is for princesses. We have to constantly practice the proper ways to curtsy—and how loudly one may properly scream when encountering a dragon or a giant."

"Do you mean even the decibel levels of screams are regulated?"

"Of course!" Penelope said with conviction. "There's much more involved than merely being an idle study."

"Any other hobbies or interests?"

"Well, uh . . . Well, I like to keep up with current affairs."

"You mean politics and social issues and sports?"

"No, not really any of that junk," Penelope sniffed. "More like who's having a romantic affair with whom. You know, *interesting* stuff."

"You mean gossip?"

"Well, yeah; I guess you *could* call it gossip, but I think the more accurate term really *is* 'current affairs.' After all, we *are* discussing the affairs that are currently going on."

"You may have a point," the prince conceded. "Have you read any good books lately?"

"Read books? What a quaint concept," Penelope said, cocking her head. Sunlight glanced off her long golden hair. Then she turned and said dismissively, "Of course not! That seems horribly boring and unladylike."

"Oh. Well, uh . . . Did you sleep well last night?"

"Thank you for asking," the princess gushed. "No, I tossed and turned all night long."

"I'm sorry to hear that. Was your bed uncomfortable or were you disturbed by some noise?"

"I had the distinct impression that there might have been a pea or pebble under the mattress that interfered with my sleep."

"You mean a pea or a pebble *under the mattress* would keep you from going to sleep?" Ron asked.

"Of course," Penelope answered matter-of-factly. "That's the way *real* princesses are."

"I'm not sure I'm following what you're saying . . ."

"Oh, you silly boy!" Penelope exclaimed. "*Everyone* knows that *real* princesses are sensitive and delicate. Why, I have developed my sensitivity to such an extent that I can often feel even grains of sand under the mattress!"

"Oh," Ron stammered. "Uh . . . Well, then, would you like me to show you around the palace, Princess Penelope?"

"Pea Pea," the princess giggled.

"Excuse me?"

"Pea Pea," she repeated. "When I was young, I had trouble saying my name: Pea-nelly-pea, but I could manage the Pea Pea part. So that's what my family and friends started calling me: Princess Pea Pea. So you may just call me Pea Pea."

"Somehow that doesn't sound quite proper."

"Nonsense. But, yes, I would like for you to show me around."

Ron gave the delicate and sensitive princess the Grand Tour of the palace grounds, the palace itself, and was showing her parts of the outer castle when a messenger informed them that it was time for lunch.

Since they were seated next to each other at lunch, the small talk continued through the meal. Finally, mercifully, Princess Pea Pea and her parents left—and Ron had time to visit with his own family.

*****

COLE BLACK RAYGUN was a monarch who was admittedly getting on up in years. Not that old King Cole particularly wanted to admit it, of course—but even his own body was reminding him of that fact with increasing frequency.

There was a time—and not too many years ago, in fact—when Cole could ride his horse all day long without thinking twice about it. Now whenever he rode for more than a few minutes, he found himself longing for a saddle with more padding. *Whatever happened to his body's natural padding where he sat down, anyway?* Heaven knows he seemed to have more than enough padding everywhere else! Why couldn't more of it be where it would do some good? Well, mark it down as being one of life's unanswered but perplexing questions.

And here was another one: When was that boy of his going to find and marry the Right Girl and get busy producing grandchildren for old King Cole to spoil? They had been pussyfooting around that issue long enough, by golly, and the king was ready to fully address the issue now that all the guests had left the castle.

"Well, son, what did you think of the princess?"

"Do you mean Princess Penelope?"

"I believe that's her name. What did you think of her?" the king repeated.

"Oh, she's rather attractive."

"Yes, I could see that part," the king answered. "But what did you think of her?"

"Uh, she seemed rather polite and mannerly. And I suppose her voice and disposition are all right."

"Confound it, boy! Answer the question! What did you think of her?"

"What do you want me to say, Dad? That she's rather attractive? I've already said it. That she's reasonably well trained in the social graces and etiquette? All right; now I've said that as well. Do you really want me to add the part about how bored I was having to be around her today?"

"What was it about her that you found so boring, Ronald?" his mother, Queen Glorianna, asked.

"Well, Mom, since it's just the three of us here, I'll answer your question honestly. But I will be most upset if anything I'm about to say ever gets repeated to anyone else. Understood?

"Why was I bored?" Prince Raygun continued. "Where should I begin? Her interests and hobbies consist primarily of crocheting, arranging flowers, embroidering, etiquette and discussing current affairs. Let me elaborate.

"*Current affairs* should not be confused with *current events*—that most *dreadful* discussion of politics, issues of public concern, warfare, sports or other such *boring* topics. Oh, no! Perish the thought! Rather, a current affair is precisely what the term says: The romantic liaisons, trysts and similar adventures among persons who are not married to each other that are currently going on. That type of current affair can occupy the princess's attention for protracted periods of time.

"Since the princess thinks books are a dreadful bore and she seems to have few identifiable intellectual skills, both she and those around her tend to get bored rather quickly. In other words, she is not the type of person I would want to be around for more than a few minutes at a time."

"Well, what about the other princesses?" the king countered. "You've met several recently."

"Yes, Dad, I have," Ron admitted. "Actually, Penelope was among the best of the princesses. It is amazing to me that monarchs who are as intelligent as most of our neighbors seem to be could produce daughters who are as vapid as the ones I've met thus far."

"Thus far?" sputtered the king. *"Thus far?* Boy, you've met every available princess. Did you catch that? *Every available princess.* All of them. Not to mention the daughters of all our nobles and aristocrats. And you apparently think you're too good for any of them."

"Dad, there must be at least a few girls of royal or noble rank who have enough intelligence to at least carry on a conversation. I know it's not impossible for them to exist. After all, *you* found one!"

Queen Glorianna tried to stifle a broad grin, but was not totally successful in doing so. Neither was her husband. The queen leaned forward and asked, "Do you mean to say that *none* of the princesses you've met were particularly intelligent?"

"Well, Anesthesia was—but she is now married to Prince Charming."

"Only because you didn't grab her while you had the chance!" King Cole exploded. "You rescued her, dag nabit! Why didn't you just go ahead and kiss her instead of taking her back to that other guy?"

"She was already betrothed to Prince Charming, Dad. Besides, I'm not sure we would have been right for each other."

"Why not?"

"We would have had trouble communicating with each other . . . since we would be unable to speak the same language."

"Wait a minute!" the king challenged. "The people of her kingdom speak the same language we do."

"Yes, Dad, the *people* speak our language—but Princess Anesthesia doesn't."

"I don't understand."

"It goes back to the wishes the good fairies made when Anesthesia was christened. Do you remember the fifth fairy's wish?"

"The fifth fairy? Uh—"

"Wasn't that the wish that she would have the grace of a flower?" asked Glorianna.

"No," answered Ron. "Having the grace of a flower was the fourth wish. The fifth wish was that she would have the voice of a nightingale."

"But nightingales produce the most beautiful music of any songbird," objected the king. "Wouldn't that wish help her to have the most splendid and beautiful voice in the land?"

"Oh, you wouldn't believe how beautiful Anesthesia's chirps and whistles are, Dad. But when it comes to carrying on a conversation in a human voice, forget it!"

"You mean . . . ?"

"Exactly!" Ron answered. "She literally has the *voice of a nightingale.* Not the voice of a human girl. A nightingale . . ."

Shyster

OLD KING COLE might have a reputation for being a merry old soul, but at the moment he was definitely not feeling particularly merry. *Frustrated* would be a more accurate word. Frustrated by that pig-headed son of his! Although the boy was heir apparent to the throne, it was not at all apparent who his bride—the future queen—would be.

Ronald had never met a girl he liked enough to date more than two or three times, much less to consider marrying. Cole and Glorianna had introduced their son to all the eligible princesses (and even a few ineligible ones) from all the neighboring kingdoms, and they had also arranged functions for the boy to meet the daughters of the kingdom's nobles and aristocrats—but Ronald had dismissed them as being too snobbish, too spoiled, too demanding, too dumb, or a combination of all of the above.

As Cole thought about the litany of girls, he smiled to himself. *The boy probably is right about them, you know.* Yes, the king knew—and he secretly sympathized. After all, who could forget the sight of that one princess who kept running around the gardens kissing all the frogs and toads?

Nevertheless, something must be done! Desperate times called for desperate action—and the king was ... well, desperate. When one is caught on the horns of a dilemma or is backed up against the wall and there is nowhere else to turn—when one is caught over the barrel and has no choice but to play the final card—when the going gets tough and it is time for the tough to get going and to make the tough decision—when one finally realizes that all the trite clichés in the world won't solve the problem but merely serve to put off the inevitable, then it must be time to do what one knows it is time to do. And, by golly, it was time for old King Cole to seize control of the situation, exert his royal authority, and make the fateful decision. After all, that was why the king was paid the big bucks.

Oh, for crying out loud! Who was he kidding? He was paid the big bucks because as king he controlled the treasury! Nevertheless, Cole knew it was time to bite the bullet, so to speak. The king would not shirk his duty. He knew what must be done. As distasteful as it might be, he would do it: Cole reluctantly sent for the royal attorney.

Lord Shyster was a middle-aged man of medium height and build with auburn hair and sharp blue eyes that constantly probed the person to whom he was speaking. Cole had the distinct impression that those eyes could see far more than Shyster ever admitted.

"You wished to see me, Your Majesty?" Lord Shyster asked.

"Yes. Did you have a chance to examine the statutes I mentioned in my message?"

"Yes, Your Majesty."

"And?"

"And they require royalty to only marry other royalty or nobility. In other words, a prince may lawfully only marry a princess, a duchess, a baroness, a countess or a lady of similar high social rank."

"Does the law provide for any exceptions?" the king asked.

"None within the law itself."

"You are implying something, my dear Lord Shyster. Outside the law . . . what?"

"You are the king. You can obviously change the law whenever you choose to do so."

"Theoretically, I could change the law," Cole responded. "But, in reality, it may prove disastrous to do so. I need—the monarchy needs—the support of my nobles, land barons and other titled gentry. Any change in the law to permit my son to avoid marrying one of their daughters might prove most difficult or embarrassing. Isn't there some other way around the law?"

"Well," the lawyer answered. "Although I did not find any exception in the law, I did find what you might call a Royal Loophole. The way people achieve the status of being nobility or aristocracy is by fiat or order of the king. Thus, you can by royal decree raise any person to the class of titled nobility.

"Think about it, Your Majesty. You have the right and power to make any man a duke, a baron, a lord or a marquis—and you can by royal fiat make any woman a duchess, a baroness, a countess, a Miss Galaxy or similar lady with high social rank.

"Sire," Lord Shyster continued, "once the boy finds the Right Girl, you can raise her to the proper social rank—and they then get married and produce grandchildren for you to spoil."

"I like it!" King Cole exclaimed. "Yes, that might work. It would at least broaden the pool—but Ronald is *so* particular and can be so difficult at times. Nevertheless, it may be worth a shot. But how can we introduce him to such girls?"

"What are the prince's favorite activities, Your Majesty?"

"Horseback riding, eating, reading books, and various sports—like fencing and archery."

"None of those activities seem particularly appropriate for meeting and sifting through a large number of girls. Maybe some type of party or social gathering might be the answer . . ."

"Do you think we could arrange a super tailgate party before the next game at the Royal Ballpark?" suggested the king.

"No, Your Majesty," answered Lord Shyster. "The players are out on strike again."

"Sometimes I think striking is the National Pastime instead of playing ball," grumbled King Cole. "Wait a minute ... wait a minute . . . That's it! We could throw a ball!"

"Uh, Your Majesty . . . I really don't see how throwing a ball around while the players are striking will allow the prince to meet a bunch of new girls."

"Not that kind of ball. I mean that we could sponsor a big fancy dance-type ball. What do you think?"

"You may have something there, Your Majesty. If every unmarried maiden over 17 or 18 years of age were invited, no one could complain that they had been left out or snubbed. Then, if Ronald does find the Right Girl, you could raise her to the proper rank without alienating the nobles and aristocracy."

"By George, we'll do it!" exclaimed the king. "Check into the possible logistics of what is involved, make a few preliminary arrangements if you need to, and get back to me later today."

A couple of hours later Lord Shyster reported back to the king. "The ball can be held here at the Palace any time you choose, but the workers will need at least three to five hours preparatory time. Either your Fiddlers Three or the Royal Philharmonic Orchestra can provide musical entertainment, while the Castle Caterers can furnish whatever refreshments you desire. The Royal Printer can have invitations printed by Wednesday, the Royal Census Bureau can get us a list of all unmarried girls and their addresses by Thursday, and the Royal Postal Service should be able to get most of the invitations delivered to the proper addresses by the end of next month."

"That's too long!" bellowed the king. "I don't want to wait any longer than a week from Saturday."

"A week from Saturday? Your Majesty, I'm afraid that's entirely out of the question. It's quite impossible! There is absolutely no way under the sun that such an elaborate dance can be staged so quickly—"

"A week from Saturday, my dear Shyster—or we may find ourselves another royal attorney. If you fail me—

"Well, you don't even want to think about what might happen to a person who fails me.

"On the other hand, if you pull it off to perfection, your reward will be one thousand gold doubloons—plus an additional 250 gold doubloons for each day before then that you move it up."

"Quite impossible, Your Majes—

"What was that you just said? Err ... uh ... you know, the more I think about it, the more I can see certain possibilities here.

"Uh, Sire, I've done a few mental calculations, and I think it just might be possible for us to stage the extravaganza you have envisioned somewhat more quickly than I first thought possible, though it will involve a few extra expenses. Let me check on a few other possible arrangements, make a few more calculations, and then I'll get back with you. Does that meet with your approval, Sire?"

"That's what I find especially interesting about lawyers," the king mused to himself. "Where there's a will, there's generally a way—and the way is often cash money. The way is also typically filled with lawyers trying to cash in. But still, they are at least experts at the Art of Possibilities."

*****

By 8:00 p.m. two days later, private couriers had delivered invitations to 98.3 percent of the unmarried maidens of marriageable age in the kingdom inviting them to a special formal ball being given in honor of Prince Ronald Raygun that Saturday night.

Vista Ridge

OPHELIA PAYNE stood on the precipice thinking about what a teacher had told her class back when she was in elementary school: "Of all the things you can overlook in life, be certain you don't overlook the overlooks that look over the Lewinsky River Valley; they offer beautiful views that should not be missed."

Of all the overlooks along Vista Ridge, this was probably Ophelia's favorite, as it provided a good view of the waterfall formed as Clinton Creek rushed over the precipice to her right and then tumbled 2350 feet to the royal blue waters of Anthony Lake in the Lewinsky River Valley below. Rising in majestic display of alpine grandeur on the opposite side of the valley were the mighty Santa Anreindeer Mountains, which rose without foothills in an unbroken sweep approximately fifteen thousand feet from the valley floor. The topmost pinnacles of Mount Killamajority were at an elevation of 17,760 feet above sea level.

Ophelia loved coming to this place, since she regarded it as one of the loveliest vistas she had ever seen. It was too bad she didn't have time to come more often. *Time!* she thought to herself. She didn't really have time to be standing here right now—but her assignment had brought her so close to this place, she just couldn't resist.

She was fortunate to have landed this job. It wasn't easy for a single mother to find part time employment that paid well. *Not easy? Ha! Impossible was more like it!* But the royal attorney was in such a hurry that he was willing to pay quite well to make certain that all these pretty invitations were promptly delivered to the girls to whom they were addressed.

Promptly! Aye, there was the rub! With one final longing gaze back at the natural grandeur she loved so much, Ophelia turned and left the scenic overlook. She had three invitations to deliver at the next address.

1703 Vista Ridge was a grand old country estate with high ivy-covered fences and a fancy wrought-iron gate. At one time there had been a guard station next to the entrance, but it appeared to have fallen into disrepair and was no longer in use.

Since the gate now stood open, Ophelia slowly drove up the private road and stopped along the circular drive that surrounded a stone statue and small dry pool in front of the big double front doors. A second glance revealed that the stone statue had once been a fountain—but, like the guard station, it did not appear to still be in use. She had to ring the doorbell twice before an attractive girl in her late teens or early twenties opened the door. The girl wore a simple dress and a soiled apron, and she held a mop in her left hand.

"May I help you?" the girl asked.

"I have three invitations that must be personally signed for," Ophelia said. "Let's see, now: They're for Miss Cynthia

Fitzgerald, Miss Zirconia Nervosa, and Miss Vampira Nervosa."

"I'm Cynthia Fitzgerald," the girl at the door responded. "Zirconia and Vampira are inside."

"Fine," Ophelia answered. "Please sign here," and she held out a computer notebook.

Cynthia signed, was handed an invitation, and beckoned Payne to come inside and follow her. Cynthia slipped the invitation into her apron pocket and led Ophelia down a large stately hallway to a set of ornate wooden doors. She knocked at one of the doors.

"What is it?" rasped a voice from inside.

"Special delivery for Zirconia and Vampira," Cynthia responded.

After a moment one of the doors opened and a lady in her late forties scowled, "You're interrupting their music lessons."

"Sorry, ma'am," Ophelia muttered as she held out the notebook. "They'll need to sign here in order to receive their invitations."

"Invitations?" the lady responded in a haughty voice. "Invitations to what?"

"Invitations to a special ball at the palace, ma'am."

At that, two awkward looking young women crowded forward, each trying to be the first to sign. A peculiar aroma wafted from them, causing Ophelia to gag and to have a sudden desire to throw up. *What was that smell, anyway?* She hadn't encountered anything like that since she had had to help unload a truck that had turned over, spilling and breaking open cases of skin softeners and hide conditioners from Crocodile Dundee, which had mixed with Bleak hair products and dyes, and both had saturated a load of Musky Oxen after shaves, deodorants and three-day pads.

Surely those girls aren't trying to use all those products at the same time! Ophelia thought to herself. She moved away from the girls and immediately felt better. *If those girls go out in public smelling like that, they may cause a nasty case of air pollution that could bring a severe reprimand from the Environmental Protection Agency.*

"Girls!" barked the lady. "You will kindly restrain yourselves until I have determined whether you should sign anything."

Turning back to Ophelia, the lady said, "Let me see one of the invitations, please." When the courier hesitated, the lady added, "I am their mother, Mrs. Madeline Nervosa Fitzgerald."

"Oh, very well," Ophelia said and handed an invitation to Mrs. Fitzgerald, who took the envelope and studied its exterior. Across the front was written:

Miss Zirconia Nervosa
1703 Vista Ridge
Santa Anreindeer District

Mrs. Fitzgerald turned over the envelope. Across the back was a splotch of red wax embossed with King Cole's seal. Glancing briefly at the courier, Mrs. Fitzgerald broke the seal, opened the envelope and removed the invitation, which had been printed on heavy white card stock. She read the words aloud:

King Cole and Queen Glorianna
Request the pleasure of your presence
At a ball honoring their son,
Crown Prince Ronald McDonald Raygun,

8:00 p.m. Saturday, the 21ˢᵗ day of May

Palace Grand Ballroom

Ignoring her daughters' gasps and giggles, Mrs. Fitzgerald announced austerely, "All right, girls, you may sign for your invitations." Turning to Cynthia, she added, "And Cinderella, when you have shown the courier to the door and have finished mopping the kitchen, report back to me."

When Zirconia and Vampira had signed their names, Ophelia handed them the invitations, took her computer notebook, and followed Cynthia back to the front door.

"Excuse me," Ophelia said. "You told me you were Cynthia Fitzgerald, but the lady who calls herself Mrs. Fitzgerald called you 'Cinderella'—and she identified the Nervosa girls as being her daughters—but not you, even though you claim to have the same last name."

"You are very observant and have a good memory; I like that," the girl smiled. "My name is Cynthia Ellen Fitzgerald, but my nickname is Cinderella. That's what everyone has called me ever since I fell into the fireplace cinders when I was a toddler. My parents were Baron and Mrs. Francis Scott "Offkey" Fitzgerald. It was my father who was the Baron—which is probably a good thing, since I wouldn't be here if Mother had been barren."

Cinderella opened the front door for Ophelia, and both ladies stepped out onto the front porch.

"Unfortunately," Cindy added, "Mom died when I was seven, and Dad remarried a few months before his own death. Madeline is my stepmother, and Zirconia and Vampira are my stepsisters. Does that answer your questions?"

"Yes," Ophelia replied. "Please forgive my asking, but part of my job is to make sure that the invitations reach the people to whom they are addressed."

"Oh, I understand," Cinderella laughed. "And thank you so very much for coming and bringing these wonderful invitations."

After closing the front door, Cinderella quickly walked back to the kitchen. She listened for a moment at the door, and then took out her own invitation and carefully read it. Its wording was identical to the one her stepmother had read aloud. Placing the invitation back inside its envelope, Cinderella thoughtfully glanced around the room, and then she kneeled down and placed the envelope under the refrigerator. Straightening up, she walked to her pan of soapy water and finished mopping the kitchen floor.

Ten minutes later Cinderella knocked at the library door.

"Come in," the raspy voice ordered. "As you heard, Zirconia and Vampira have been invited to the royal ball for Prince Ronald Raygun on Saturday. As their mother, I also intend to be there. But that means that you will need to help get the three of us ready for the ball. We will need to choose our gowns—and they may have to be cleaned or altered.

"You will also need to arrange for a coach or limo to come for us. Check on the prices and arrangements and report back to me for confirmation. And all of this is in addition to your regular chores and duties, of course. Do you understand what is required?"

"Yes ma'am," Cinderella replied. "I'll get right on it."

When Cinderella had called all the coaches and limo services in the area, she reported back to her stepmother, who made her selection. Cinderella then called and confirmed the order.

Zirconia, Vampira and Madeline tried on at least eight formal gowns apiece before deciding which attire would be most appropriate for the upcoming ball at the palace. Cinderella helped make minor alterations as needed—plus she also did such normal chores as cooking the family's meals, sweeping the floors, and washing both the dirty dishes and the soiled clothes.

It was not until Cinderella went to bed that first night after receiving the invitation that she had any time for herself. Removing a loose board from the floor under her bed, Cinderella pulled out a formal gown that had belonged to her mother, and which she had hidden away about the time her father remarried. Since Cinderella was no longer permitted to wear fine clothing or jewels, she had kept the dress hidden inside a blanket in her special hiding place. Although the gown was wrinkled and would require a few minor alterations, Cinderella was thrilled to see how close it came to fitting her. As she held the dress up in front of her reflected image in the mirror, she thought, *Yes! I can do this. There's no reason I can't be ready by Saturday evening.*

*****

Cinderella said nothing to the other members of the household. Instead, she worked hard to finish all her chores and to help her stepmother, Zirconia and Vampira get ready for the ball on Saturday. When they were all ready and waiting for the coach to arrive, Cinderella slipped off to her room and changed into her mother's gown. She quickly brushed her hair and then ran back downstairs, catching up with the others just as they were climbing into their coach.

"Wait here for us, coachman," ordered Madeline Fitzgerald. "Girls, come with me for just a moment," she said to the others as she walked stoically back into the house.

"Just what do you think you are doing?" demanded the stepmother.

"I . . . I thought I was going to the ball with the rest of the family."

"You!" exclaimed Zirconia. "You—a mere housekeeper—going to Prince Raygun's ball?"

"Oh, that's rich!" chimed in Vampira as she pretended to dance with Zirconia. "Here, king, would you please hold my mop and broom so that I can dance with your son?"

"I admit that I do all the housework around here—but that doesn't mean I'm any less a member of the family," Cinderella insisted.

"*You*—a member of the family? Where do you get that preposterous idea?" asked Vampira.

"Well, this house belonged to my father before he died, and the wealth you so freely spend on yourselves was also his. And I was his only child."

"Yes, what you say is true," replied Madeline coldly. "But when your father died, I inherited all that he had: his wealth, his debt, everything. I have looked after you and have made sure you had food to eat and a comfortable place to sleep. *I* determine how the money should be spent, and *I will not tolerate insolence* directed toward *my* daughters. Do you understand?"

"Please forgive me. I wasn't trying to be insolent, stepmother. You are the only family I have, and I—"

"I do **not** consider you to be family," Madeline snapped. "I tolerate you and I look after you. But you are *not* family—and you are never to be so presumptuous as to claim that status again. Is that understood?"

"Yes, stepmother."

"Now where did you get that dress?"

"It was my mother's before she died. I've had it put up all these years."

"Your mother's, eh? Well, your father inherited everything your mother owned. And then I inherited everything that belonged to your father. That means the dress you are wearing belongs to me. Take it off."

"Wh ... what?" Cinderella stammered.

"I said *take it off!*" Madeline barked. Turning to Zirconia and Vampira, she purred, "Girls, Cinderella either seems to have developed a problem with her hearing or she is being stubborn and obstinate again. Help me remove my dress from her body."

As Cinderella mutely stood in shocked and embarrassed silence, Madeline, Zirconia and Vampira attacked the dress with gusto, ripping the beautiful gown to shreds.

They then turned around haughtily and stalked back to the waiting coach, leaving Cinderella alone—shocked, embarrassed, and frustrated.

The Godfather

As the shock wore off, Cinderella first felt rage at the extreme injustice of the entire situation. Then the rage subsided as a deep sense of hopeless depression overwhelmed her like a monumental tsunami. Cinderella collapsed into a pool of tears, crying so hard she felt that her heart would literally explode.

"Oh, dear Lord," she cried. "I had saved Mother's gown for all these years; it was the only possession I had to remind me of her—and now it's gone. Even worse is the knowledge that... that they don't even care for me. I knew they abused me and didn't really show love and affection—but I kept hoping that . . ."

Sobs interrupted her thoughts until she was able to recompose herself, choke back her tears, and continue.

"Where should I go? What should I do? Is there even a purpose for my life? Please help me, Lord. Let me know your will and what I should do."

Cinderella was crying so much that she did not hear the doorbell ringing at first. Although she felt very much like either ignoring the bell or shouting "go away" to the unknown intruder, it was not in her nature to be rude. She therefore reluctantly got up, wrapped the remnants of her gown around her as well as she could, tried to dry her tears, and did her best to compose herself.

When Cinderella opened the front door, she was confronted by a slightly overweight man in an immaculate suit. He appeared to be around sixty years old, his hair was thinning but perfectly groomed, and his jowls drooped a little.

"Hello, Cinderella," he said.

"Hello," she answered meekly. "You seem to know me, but I'm afraid I don't recognize you."

"You mean you don't know who I am?" remarked the man with a slightly amused smile.

"No. Should I?"

"I'm your fairy godfather, and I'm here to help you."

"Fair ... *fairy godfather?*" Cinderella stammered. "You ... er ... you don't look much like a fairy to me."

"What do I look like to you?"

"Well," Cinderella answered. "You're sort of a cross between Richard Nixon and Marlon Brando."

A slight frown creased the godfather's brow. "I'm not sure whether that's a compliment or an insult."

Then his countenance lightened as he smiled and said, "Well, either way, let me make one thing perfectly clear: Although I am neither of those two gentlemen, at this point in time I am here to make you an offer you can't refuse."

"What kind of offer?"

"You want to go to the palace ball for Ronald Raygun, don't you?"

"Yes."

"Well, I'm here to make it possible."

"But they tore my mother's gown," Cinderella protested. "Even if I could manage to get to the palace, I have nothing to wear."

"Never fear," the godfather responded. "I just happen to have with me a Neiman-Marcus catalog. You may have anything you want from it."

"Really? Do you really and truly mean it?"

"Yes. I really and truly do mean it."

"Oh, Godfather! That's wonderful!" Cinderella exclaimed as she tore through the catalog with an enthusiasm that would rival that of her stepsisters as they tore through her dress. "Let's see now: I think I'll take this .... and this ...... and this ... and this, and this and this and this and this and ... "

"Whoa, girl! Just one gown, one necklace, one set of earrings, and one pair of shoes," interjected the fairy godfather.

"Oh, all right. Let's see, now . . . I think I'll take this Calvin Klein evening gown, this Johannes De Beers diamond necklace, these Emmett Smith diamond earrings, and the Neiman-Marcus genuine alligator leather slippers with double-lined silken interiors."

"Very good!" exclaimed the fairy godfather as he made some entries on his laptop computer. "You made some excellent choices—except that I thought that the script called for glass slippers."

"Too impractical," responded Cinderella. "I don't think they would be as comfortable as what I chose, I would not be able to dance as well in them, and glass slippers are just too breakable."

"Are you sure?"

"Certainly! Haven't you ever seen the Disney version?"

A few minutes later a sleigh landed outside the house and an even more overweight bearded man in a red and white outfit brought in the requested items. He handed a computerized tablet to the godfather, who signed in the designated area.

The bearded man presented the items to Cinderella, who tried them on. After making sure everything was a perfect fit, the bearded man left again in his sleigh.

"Ho! Ho! Ho!" he cheerfully called out as he disappeared from sight.

Cinderella momentarily froze. *Was he calling her a ho? No, probably not.*

"Thank you ever so much, fairy godfather," said Cinderella as she looked at herself in a mirror.

Cinderella kissed her fairy godfather lightly on his cheek, turned to go, and then stopped short. Turning back with a quizzical look, she said, "Uh ... fairy godfather—I just realized something: The palace is twenty-five miles from here. How am I going to get there?"

"Hmmmmmmm," mused the godfather. "Neiman's doesn't have any coaches, limos or other transportation—so I guess we'll just have to use magic. What do you have around here that I can work with?"

"Well," answered Cinderella. "I just so happen to have a pumpkin, a dog and some mice."

"Perfect!" exclaimed the godfather. And with a wave of his magic wand, he muttered the Magic Words[3], and the dog was changed into a chauffeur, the

---

[3] which we can't print here, of course, since those words have been copyrighted.

pumpkin became a magnificent golden Lincoln Continental limousine, and the mice were turned into gasoline.

"Are you sure it's all right to use mice for fuel?" asked Cinderella.

"Of course, Honey," answered the godfather. "If BP can put oil on your clams and Exxon can put a tiger in your tank, surely we can use a few mice."

With another wave of his wand, the fairy godfather created an elegant hairstyle for Cinderella, who kissed him again and exclaimed, "This is just like a dream — a wonderful, unbelievably marvelous dream!"

"Yes, my dear. But like all dreams, I'm afraid that this one will also have to end somewhat sooner than you might wish," warned the godfather. "You only have until midnight to enjoy all these things from Neiman-Marcus—and then they will disappear."

"Why?"

"Because if I don't get these items retagged and back to Neiman-Marcus before the store opens tomorrow morning, there could be serious problems. The gown must also be cleaned and pressed, while the jewelry must be put back into their display cases. Since the shoes can't be returned after being worn, you may keep them.

Also, there's the fact that the magic I used on the pumpkin, dog and mice expires at midnight."

"Why's that?"

"The collective bargaining agreement that allows fairy godmothers and godfathers to temporarily bless our godchildren requires that any magic used must expire no later than midnight of the day when such magic was utilized. You do understand what that means, don't you? You need to be back here before the magic expires, since it would be a long tiring journey if you had to walk all the way from the palace."

"Yes," responded Cinderella. "I understand—and I promise to do as you have asked. It is so much more than I could ever have hoped for. Thank you so very much."

As Cinderella got into the car to leave for the palace ball, she wondered, *Am I stepping out of the frying pan into the fire? I've already been rejected and badly burned here...in what should have been the safety of my own home. How much worse might it be in the uncaring world of the palace rulers and bureaucrats?*

The Palace Ball

PRINCE RONALD RAYGUN leaned against the parapet that enclosed the palace's veranda. The full moon gave a soft glow to the Santa Anreindeer Mountains in the distance. The sounds of the Royal Philharmonic Orchestra filtered through Ron's consciousness as his mother ambled up to him.

"Why are you out here, Ronnie?" she asked.

"Oh, I've met and danced with all the girls who have shown up for the ball, and—well, I guess I just needed a breath of fresh air."

"Don't tell me that pretty girls tire you out that much!"

"Not really," the prince confessed. "It's just that there was something about the last couple of girls that made me want to catch my breath."

"What was that?"

"Well, there was this peculiar aroma about them."

"Perfume?"

"Not exactly. Actually, Mom, they have an extremely bad case of B. O., and they seem incredibly dumb. Apparently, all they do is sit around watching *Dates of Our Wives* on TV. Oh, sure, I've met plenty of girls out there tonight. But about half of them appear to be big game hunters intent on bagging me. The other half seem to be here either out of curiosity or so they can brag to their friends and acquaintances that they have danced with Prince Raygun.

"I haven't met a single girl yet who seems interested in me as *a person.* I don't want to merely be a prize to be won—or a celebrity or other freak to be stared at. Can't anyone here just see me as a real human being who also has hopes and dreams—and doubts and fears? Well, I tried to tell Dad that I didn't think this was the best way to meet the Right Girl."

"Maybe some of the formality and awe of being in the Royal Palace will have worn off by the next round of dances. Who knows? You might find someone who has the qualities that are especially important to you."

"I hope so, Mother," Ron sighed as he turned to go back inside. "I certainly hope so."

Queen Glorianna watched her son take a deep breath and steel himself before once again assuming a regal bearing and an air of confidence as he walked briskly back into the ballroom. The queen followed a few paces behind her son, and then joined her husband on a raised dais at the end of the ballroom opposite the orchestra.

"I think I know what is troubling our son," she confided to her husband. "He seems to envision the young ladies as having invisible fishing poles—and he is the fish most of them are trying to catch."

"I hadn't thought of it that way," remarked the king, "but he's probably right."

The second round of dances was well under way when Cinderella arrived at the Palace. She followed the sound of music to the Grand Ballroom, where she stood transfixed at the top of the steps leading onto the dance floor below. Scores of girls in gorgeous gowns stood around the sides of the ballroom, while the dance floor was filled with couples dancing to the beat of the music. When the waltz ended, the couples stepped apart.

Ronald Raygun had just finished dancing with a beautiful young lady who seemed to fulfill every dumb blond joke he had ever heard when he spotted Cinderella looking around the room from the top step. On an impulse, Prince Raygun walked up to her, bowed slightly, and asked, "May I help you, miss?"

"Thank you," she smiled. "I received an invitation to attend a ball here at the Palace, but I was not sure where I should go."

"Well," laughed the prince, "as you can see, we are dancing the night away. And since neither of us seems to have a partner at the moment, would you care to have the next dance?"

"I would love to," answered Cinderella.

As Ron took Cinderella's hand, she asked him, "Well, when you're not helping to run the country, what do you especially like to do?"

"Oh, all sorts of things."

"Such as?"

"Games, sports, reading, movies, you name it," he answered.

"What books do you especially like?"

"I guess that depends on whether I'm reading for business or for pleasure. If I'm trying to improve my skills, I lean toward self-help books, political theory, biographies or philosophy. On the other hand, if I'm reading for pleasure, I generally like to curl up with a good mystery or adventure story."

"Which are your favorites?"

"That's hard to say, since there are so many good books." The prince twirled Cinderella through a couple of waltz steps as he thought a few moments. Then he held her a bit closer as he replied, "I especially liked some of the classics like

Sherlock Holmes and Jack London. But then again, I also enjoy some of the newer works by Clancy, Grissom, Thoene, Wibberley, Collins, and Rowling. How about you?"

"Probably my favorite Sherlock Holmes would be *Hound of the Baskervilles.*"

"That's my favorite, too."

"Although *The Call of the Wild* may be London's most famous book, I personally liked *White Fang* better."

Prince Raygun thought a moment and then nodded, "I think you're right."

"One of my favorite classics is *Jane Eyre.*"

"I started to read that once, but lost interest."

"You probably didn't get into it far enough. It takes a while to really get going. But it presents one of the most interesting moral dilemmas I've ever read."

"I may have to give it another try. Do you ever read nonfiction?"

"Of course."

"What's your favorite?"

"As a great man once said," and Cinderella dropped her voice an octave as she mimicked the prince, "That's hard to say, since there are so many good books."

"Hey!" Ron laughed. "No fair throwing my words back at me!"

"Oh? Where would you prefer that I throw them?" asked Cinderella as she pretended to look around for a place to chunk the words.

"Well, at least I answered your question."

"Fair enough. Since I usually read nonfiction to learn information or to answer a question I might have, the topics and authors vary substantially from time to time. Other than the Bible, I guess the nonfiction work that gave me the most food for thought would be *The Science of God* by Dr. Gerald Schroeder."

Ron stopped his dance step so quickly that Cinderella tripped over his left foot. He caught her, held her in front of him, looked into her eyes intently, and said, "I think you're serious."

"What's wrong?"

"That's not the type of book I would expect a beautiful young lady to be reading."

"Why not?"

"I ... er ... I don't know," the prince stammered. "It's just not."

"Are you so chauvinistic as to presume girls can't be mentally stimulated by great literature or by thought provoking analysis?"

"Whoa, girl. I didn't mean to upset you. Your response just caught me off guard; that's all. By the way, you haven't introduced yourself."

"Whoops, sorry. I'm Cinderella."

"Cinderella. That's rather pretty."

"Thank you."

"Wait here a moment, Cinderella," Ron said as their dance ended. He walked over to King Cole and told him, "Dad, I want to visit with this girl a bit more. Would you please have the Royal Guardsmen dance with the other girls so that they will be entertained?"

A pleased expression quickly replaced King Cole's surprised look as he responded, "Of course, son."

Then Ron led Cinderella out onto the veranda, where they continued to dance in a more private setting.

"Do you ever read political theory?" he asked.

"Occasionally."

"Which ones?"

"Locke, Hobbes, Jefferson, Wilde, Morris, Gingrich, and several others."

"If you've read all of those, I'd say you do more than 'occasional' reading."

"My father built a wonderful well-stocked library at our house, and some of my fondest memories are of being cuddled up in his lap as he read those books. After he died, his library became my sanctuary where I could go after I had finished my chores. Those books became my friends and advisors."

"Which do you especially prefer?"

"Some aspects of *Utopia* and socialism sound alluring and attractive, but they have tended to not work out as well when tried in the real world. I think the theories of Locke, Hobbes and Jefferson tend to be more practical and to work better. What do you think?"

"I think you summarized my conclusions quite succinctly."

"You mean the crown prince in a monarchy is a fan of democracy and individual freedoms?"

"A monarch who properly does his job should be concerned with the welfare of the people he governs," the prince answered. "And there is no reason individual rights and freedoms cannot exist in a monarchy."

"Well spoken, Sire," Cinderella murmured as she leaned against Ron. She found herself enjoying the gentle caress of this handsome prince. His touch seemed to melt away her cares and anxieties, and she discovered that he had a sharp intellect, a quick wit, and a probing mind.

Thank you, Lord, Cinderella silently prayed. *Thank you for making this enchanted evening possible. I may not know what the future holds for me, but now I can face it with greater confidence.*

For his part, Ron was fascinated to finally meet a beautiful young lady whose mind and intellect matched her lovely figure, and who also enjoyed reading and thinking. Cinderella easily engaged him in conversation and seemed to be genuinely interested in what he had to say. She was warm and friendly, and he found the touch of her hands and the feel of her body to be as stimulating as the way she touched him mentally and emotionally.

As they danced, they visited about their hopes and dreams, favorite foods and sports, books and movies they especially liked, their beliefs and philosophies, and about many other things. The minutes melted away. By this time, they were no longer dancing, but were rather walking hand in hand through the Royal Gardens. It was there in the Royal Gardens that Cinderella heard the clock begin to strike[4] the twelve gongs that would signal midnight.

"Oh, where did the time go?" Cinderella gasped with a horrified expression.

---

[4] Pop quiz: Briefly explain [500 words or less] the difference between the striking clock and the striking ball players. Mail your answer to the National Labor Relations Board.

"What's wrong?"

"I have an early curfew, and promised I'd leave the palace for home by midnight. I've had the most glorious evening of my life—but I have to go now."

"No, wait—"

"I'm sorry," cried Cinderella as she broke into a run.

"Wait," called the prince after her. "Where *is* your home? How will I ever find you?"

Cinderella didn't pause to answer as she ran back through the Palace. As Prince Raygun tried to follow her, he was intercepted by the other girls, who were desperate for one last chance at the prince. By the time Ron succeeded in getting through the throng, Cinderella had driven off in the Lincoln limousine. The only tangible reminder the prince had of Cinderella was one Neiman-Marcus genuine alligator leather slipper with double-lined silken interior, which had slipped off Cindy's foot as she ran away.

Cinderella would not have gone far in her Lincoln limo except that she had forgotten that the kingdom was on

Daylight Confusion Time. However, the condition of the streets and highways was such that it took her the entire extra hour to go the twenty-five miles from the Palace to her home. Thus, about the time she got back to the private drive in front of her house, the car suddenly disappeared and Cinderella found herself sitting on the driveway with a dog, a pumpkin and parts of several mice. Cindy hid the pumpkin, ran into the house, and changed out of her clothes so that her fairy godfather could take them back to Neiman-Marcus.

*****

Back at the Palace, the dancing had ceased and King Cole and Prince Ronald personally gave each girl a golden necklace as a memento of their evening at the Palace, and thanked each of them for coming. Then the king, queen, and prince joined Lord Shyster in the king's chambers to discuss the proceedings that had occurred that evening.

The Quest

THE KING'S CHAMBERS were a set of rooms sequestered next to the royal bedroom on the second floor of the Palace. The principal room consisted of his private library, his personal work desk, and several large comfortable chairs and sofas. Although the rich mahogany, walnut and oak paneling gave the room a dignified air, it was not as formal as the rooms on the first floor.

King Cole motioned for the others to be seated, but he chose to stand. He started to walk toward his desk, but then turned and bellowed, "It was a disaster! Do you hear me? An unmitigated disaster! I haven't had something turn out this poorly since Humpty Dumpty went to pieces at a big reception several years ago. All my horses and all my men couldn't put Humpty back together again!"

"If your men needed competent assistance in their efforts with Lord Humpty, they should have asked their ladies for help instead of their horses," muttered Queen Glorianna. "Those horses just kept messing things up worse."

"Only one lass out of all those pretty girls seemed to even interest you—and then she took off like a sprinter at the Olympics!" the king continued. "What did you say or do to cause that type of reaction?"

"Nothing, Dad. She heard the clock start to chime, thanked me for a wonderful evening, said she had to run—and then she did."

"You didn't try something unseemly with her?"

"No. Of course not."

"She just decided to run out on you?"

"She said she had an early curfew and had to get home."

King Cole thought for a moment and then commented, "Well, maybe it was a blessing in disguise that she did vanish."

"Just what do you mean by that remark?" his son demanded.

"Think about it. What could possibly cause this mysterious lady of yours to suddenly disappear at the end of the evening? Maybe she's already married. Maybe she was a witch or a spy or something. In any event, it appears she had ***something*** to hide. Unless, of course, she suffers from hopelessly unstable mood changes or some other mental problem."

"Or maybe," the prince suggested pointedly, "when she gives her word to someone—such as to be back home at a particular time—she keeps her word."

"You really like her, don't you?" Queen Glorianna asked softly.

"Yes, Mother, I do. In fact, I think she is the most wonderful girl I have ever met."

"Do you love her?"

"Well, one night is too soon to know if it's really love or simply infatuation."

Ron stood silently and thought for a moment before continuing. "Yes—yes, I think I may very well love her. Somehow, somehow in my heart I know she's right for me—but I need more time to make certain my head agrees with my heart."

"How are you going to find her again?"

"She told me her name was Cinderella and that she received an invitation to the ball. A search of the Royal Census Bureau records should help us narrow down the list somewhat. Our pursuit party said her golden limousine was initially heading northeast when she left here—but they lost track of her when they were cut off by a large group of reporters who were chasing a white Ford Bronco going the other way. I also have one of her shoes. Here, Lord Shyster, what do you make of it?"

"Well," responded the royal attorney as he examined the shoe, "it appears to be a rather new alligator leather shoe . . . "

Lord Shyster turned the shoe over and examined the interior. "Ah, yes, here are the measurements and other markings: Yes, it is a Neiman-Marcus genuine alligator leather slipper with double-lined silken interior for the left foot, lady's size 13. Wow! That's definitely a big shoe! In fact, it's even larger than what I wear."

Shyster sighed before continuing. "This has to be a special-order shoe, since I've never seen a lady have such big feet. Of course, she was taller than most of the other girls at the ball, if I recall correctly. Our best bet would probably be to contact Neiman-Marcus and find out who purchased the size 13 lady's alligator leather slippers with double-lined silken interiors."

But Neiman-Marcus had no record of even carrying that shoe in a size 13, much less of ever selling it to anyone. And the Royal Census Bureau listed no one whose name was Cinderella.

"Of course," said the clerk at the Census Bureau, "Cinderella could be just a nickname. And with regard to your other request, the Royal Census Bureau does *not* keep any information on foot sizes."

*****

Ronald Raygun was desperate. He had finally met the girl of his dreams[5]—only to

---

[5] Not only was she the girl of his dreams, but she was also the girl he had danced with at the Royal Ball—and he really, really liked her.

lose her. He pondered his options, and then sent for the royal attorney.

"Lord Shyster, I have decided to send you on a quest for Cinderella."

"Do you know where she is?"

"No, but we know she wore this shoe."

"Ah, yes. So you want me to go throughout the kingdom and try this size 13 Neiman-Marcus genuine alligator leather slipper with double-lined silken interior on every maiden's foot until I find the right one. Right?"

"I thought it was the left foot."

"You're right. So you want me to try it on every maiden's left foot until I find the right foot."

"That's right. And hopefully, the right left foot will also belong to the Right Girl."

*****

Lord Shyster was most anxious to find the mysterious disappearing lady—not only because he liked the Royal Family and wanted his clients to be happy, but also because his own fee for putting together the Royal Ball was largely contingent upon King Cole's being satisfied with the result. Cinderella's limousine had last been seen heading northeast from the Palace. Lord Shyster therefore decided to begin searching in that direction. Eventually he arrived at 1703 Vista Ridge in the Santa Anreindeer District.

Since Cinderella had been locked in her room by her stepmother, only Zirconia and Vampira were downstairs to try on the slipper. But Vampira's left foot—like that of every other maiden the attorney had seen—was far too small to fill the shoe offered to her.

"My goodness!" cried Zirconia when she tried on the shoe. "This thing is almost as big as the clodhoppers Cinderella wears!"

Lord Shyster perked up. "What did you say?"

"The only women's shoes I have ever seen that were this big are the monsters Cinderella wears."

"Who is this Cinderella?"

"Oh, nothing at all, My Lord," said Madeline Fitzgerald. "Just a silly slip of the tongue."

"Woman, please sit down and let your precious daughter answer my question," the lawyer commanded as he gently took Zirconia's hand and lifted her to her feet. "You do know who this Cinderella is, don't you?"

"Sure I do," replied Zirconia. "She's our maid and housekeeper. She cleans our house and cooks our food and does all the work around here."

"Where is she right now?"

"I don't know. She has to be around here somewhere. Probably in her room."

"I'll give you 100 gold doubloons if you'll take me to her."

"A hundred gold doubloons?" Zirconia responded, pumping the attorney's hand enthusiastically. "Mister, you've got yourself a deal!"

Zirconia led Lord Shyster to Cinderella's room in the attic, but they discovered that the door was locked.

"Who has the key?" asked the royal attorney.

"She must have locked herself into her room, Milord," Madeline answered.

"No, I didn't," Cinderella cried from inside her room. "You locked me in here so I couldn't try on my slipper."

"Unlock that door," commanded Lord Shyster. Then he added with a grin, "Or I'll huff and I'll puff and I'll blow the door down."

"You shouldn't make idle threats, Milord."

"I'm a lawyer," he answered. "I never make threats I can't back up. And I assure you that I have more than enough power to deal with a minor inconvenience like a locked door—or with you, for that matter. You will either open that door—now—or I will use my magic cellular telephone to call in whatever additional force I choose."

"That won't be necessary," Madeline sighed as she pulled the key from her pocket and unlocked the door. Cinderella got up from the floor where she had been kneeling while looking through the keyhole. She took a few uncertain steps toward the group of people gathered outside her bedroom door.

"Hello, Cinderella," smiled Lord Shyster as he produced the slipper. "If the shoe fits, wear it."

The attorney bent down and held the shoe for Cinderella, who slid her left foot into the slipper. The shoe did indeed fit ... perfectly.

"Are you really happy living in a house where they lock you in your attic room?" he asked.

"Are you kidding me?" Cinderella replied. "Both my parents died in this house. I have been beaten and mistreated by my stepmother, ridiculed and mocked by my stepsisters, and treated as a servant. All I do all day long is make the beds, clean and mop the floors, cook and serve the meals, wash the dishes and clothes, and do whatever else is needed to satisfy my stepmother and stepsisters. In short, this house has too many painful memories."

"Let me see what I can do about that," the attorney said as he pulled out his cell phone and called a number.

"Hello, Ronald?" Shyster spoke into the phone. "I found her. Yes, yes, she's fine. No, she lives in the Santa Anreindeer District. She allegedly is the maid and housekeeper of a country estate beside Clinton Creek that overlooks Anthony Lake and the Lewinsky River valley—

"Ha! Very good, sir. Would you like for me to bring her with me back to the Palace?

"Okay, will do. Is there a private room she could use there? If so, I could have her bring her things as well.

"Great. All right. Here she is," and he handed the phone to Cinderella.

"Hello?" she asked. "I'm sorry I had to run out so suddenly. I didn't even get to tell you what a wonderful time I had. Please forgive me . . .

"Thank you so very much . . .

"Yes, thank you—but there's something you should know if you don't already. I'm not royalty or aristocracy or anything else that's special . . .

"Oh, that's so sweet of you . . .

"That would be wonderful. Are you sure it will be all right with your parents? What? The king suggested it? Oh, wow! That's fantastic! Okay, I'll see you then."

Turning to Lord Shyster, Cinderella added, "He wants to talk to you again."

"Sounds like a good plan, Chief," Shyster said. "What? King Cole said to put it all on his account? That's awfully generous of him—well, a lot more generous than he sometimes is, anyway. All right, we'll see you in a few hours, then."

Turning to his chauffeur, Lord Shyster said, "Help Cinderella load up her things. Give me the keys and I'll take a load out to the car and get the hundred gold doubloons I promised this other young lady for bringing me to Cinderella's room."

He then told Cinderella, "Load up everything you want to take. I am to take you shopping for new things, which will then be moved to the Palace. The king and queen have made a guest room available for your use for at least the time being. Prince Ronald and I only know you as Cinderella—but that is apparently just a nickname. What is your full legal name? And your parents' names?"

"My legal name is Cynthia Ellen Fitzgerald, and my parents were Francis Scott and Christina Fitzgerald."

"Thank you. Have I spelled the names correctly?"

"Yes. That's right," Cinderella said. "Oh, here's the other slipper I wore to the Ball. Do you want to keep both of them or should I keep them?"

"Just pack them both into your bags, Cinderella. By the way, when I told the prince that you were allegedly the maid and housekeeper, he answered that you were his Sweeping Beauty, since you had already swept him off his feet."

"That sounds like something he'd say," Cinderella laughed. "He is so very, very sweet ... and charming."

Later that same day Cinderella moved into the Palace. Lord Shyster revealed that while he had taken Cindy shopping, he had also been having his legal staff searching the real property and probate records of the kingdom—and Cynthia Ellen Fitzgerald was the true legal owner of the house and land known as 1703 Vista Ridge and of various funds that they were still trying to track down. He quietly confided to King Cole that since Cinderella's father was Baron Francis Scott "Offkey" Fitzgerald, the king would not even need to use the Royal Loophole they had earlier discussed . . . should events progress as they hoped.

Over the next several months Cinderella and Prince Ronald spent much of their waking hours together. The feelings they had for each other continued to grow until both were sure that they truly did love each other. It was shortly after that point in time that Ronald Raygun ceased being the kingdom's most eligible bachelor—and became one of its most happily married men.

Cinderella also found that being married to her wonderful prince was a vast improvement. Thus, they both lived happily ever after ... well, that is ... all except for one minor detail.

Because of a downturn in the economy and decreased revenues, the kingdom had to outsource some jobs and downsize the staff of servants and attendants in the castle.

Consequentially, Cinderella discovered that even though she was married to the crown prince of the kingdom and was in line to become the future queen, she still had to make the beds, clean and mop the floors, cook and serve the meals, and wash the dishes and clothes.

But at least the Royal Library was extremely well stocked with books and movies—and she and her handsome prince had almost as much fun together there as they did in certain other parts of the castle.

Ronald Raygun and the Sweeping Beauty is available as a play for school or community theater.

Sweeping Beauty

**If you enjoyed
Ronald Raygun and the Sweeping Beauty,
read on for a preview of**

Wizard's Gambit

**A science fiction / fantasy novel
by Bill Kincaid**

Available on Amazon.com and Kindle

Jackzen awakened from a sound sleep when his wife clutched his arm and fearfully asked, "What was that?"

"What's what?" His voice was groggy, but his muscles tensed.

They both listened intently for a moment, clutching each other in the predawn darkness.

"That!" Annika responded as a crash from the front room was quickly followed by the sound of loud footsteps rushing toward their bedroom, accompanied by the light of four burning torches.

Jackzen tossed aside the covers and started to spring from the bed, but was immediately forced back by a spear that cut him in his chest. He dropped onto the bed, clutching the top bedspread to his chest to stanch the bleeding. Only then did he look at the men surrounding him.

Soldiers. Or enforcers. Armed, surly, and mean.

"What's the meaning of this outrage?" he demanded.

"We're here to collect what you owe the Crown," responded one of them, a tall burly man standing to the right of the one who held the spear that had wounded him.

"We've already paid everything we owe the king," Jackzen protested. "All taxes and fees that were due, plus the extra assessments that enforcers demanded."

"That's what you claim," the enforcer who was apparently in charge replied. "We say you haven't paid what you owe."

"Kratzl!" Jackzen swore. "I can prove I paid it."

"Let's see your proof."

"Let me get up, and I'll get my receipt."

The officer motioned for his men to allow Jackzen to rise from the bed. Still holding the bedspread against his chest, Jackzen made his way to his dresser, rummaged through a drawer, and withdrew the vital document. He handed it to the officer triumphantly.

The officer read it carefully by the light of one of the torches, and then burned it in the fire.

"What other proof do you have to offer?"

"Hey!" Jackzen objected. "You can't do that!"

"I just did. What other proof do you have?"

"I shouldn't need any other proof. That receipt showed I paid all charges in full."

"Receipt? I don't see any receipt." The officer turned to his men. "Do any of you see a receipt?"

They laughed, sneered, and shook their heads.

"What proof do you now have to offer?"

Jackzen sputtered but held his tongue. "What is it you want?" he asked.

"I want your teenage daughter."

"Marza? Why?"

"Come off it, Jackzen. You're smarter than that. You know why."

"No! You have no right!" Jackzen yelled while lunging at the officer before being clubbed over the head by another enforcer.

"We have all the rights," Jackzen heard as he slipped from consciousness. "We're the king's enforcers."

Other Books by Bill Kincaid

Historical Fiction:

Nicodemus' Quest—The Jewish Supreme Court known as the Sanhedrin had already found Jesus guilty of blasphemy and condemned him to die, setting in motion the events culminating in his death by crucifixion a few hours later. Why then would two of the most influential members of the Sanhedrin risk alienating their colleagues by removing Jesus' body from the cross and giving hi a proper burial? Didn't they realize it was a lost cause—that Jesus' death proved he couldn't be either the Messiah or the Son of God?

Yet Nicodemus and Joseph of Arimathea risked their reputations and everything they had worked so hard to accomplish throughout their lives by identifying with Jesus at a time when even his friends and disciples had deserted him.

What had they learned in their investigations into Jesus' background and ministry that caused them to take such drastic action? For that matter, why had they investigated him in the first place? Is Jesus the Messiah? And what relevance does that have for us two thousand years later?

Saul's Quest—Saul of Tarsus appeared to have an extremely bright future. He had distinguished himself as being the star pupil of Gamaliel, who was considered the outstanding first century teacher in Israel. Although still a young man, Saul had already been accepted as a member of both the Pharisees and of the Sanhedrin, the principal legislative and judicial body of Israel.

Now the Jewish high priest has given Saul the assignment of hunting down, arresting, and persecuting the men and women who claim that Jesus of Nazareth is both the Messiah and the Son of God. Saul pursued the task with his usual dedication and determination . . . until something unusual happens on the road to Damascus. Walk with Saul on his momentous journey that radically changed not only his life, but also the history of the world.

Joseph's Quest— Are you facing problems, obstacles, or challenges in your life? Does it feel as if you've been broken beyond repair? Are you in need of a friend? Or a helping hand? Or a role model?

Meet Joseph. He was betrayed by his own jealous brothers, who dropped him into a pit while they considered whether to kill him. He was sold into slavery and later unjustly accused and wrongfully imprisoned.

But his true story shows it is possible to overcome the problems, obstacles and challenges of life and eventually come out on top.

All titles are available on Amazon.com and Kindle

Made in the USA
Middletown, DE
28 July 2024

58068790R00071